THE LEGEND OF
SLEEPY HOLLOW

ISBN-13: 978-0-8249-5603-5

Published by Ideals Children's Books
An imprint of Ideals Publications
A Guideposts Company
Nashville, Tennessee
www.idealsbooks.com

Color separations by Precision Color Graphics, Franklin, Wisconsin
Printed and bound in China

Library of Congress CIP data on file

Leo_Jun10_2

Designed by Marisa Jackson

The paintings by Russ Flint were rendered in oils.

THE LEGEND OF
SLEEPY HOLLOW

Adapted from the original
by Washington Irving

With oil paintings by
Russ Flint

ideals children's books.
Nashville, Tennessee

On the eastern bank of the lazy Tappan Zee River, nestled between two mountain peaks, rests the small valley of Sleepy Hollow, which abounds with strange and wonderful happenings. Most remarkable of these is the legend of the ghost who haunts the region.

The ghost is said to wear a long, woolen cape, like a trooper from the Revolutionary War. Each night, he leaves his churchyard grave and hurries to the site of a long-forgotten battle. Riding his huge horse, the ghost is a body in frantic search of his head—lost in a raging battle. He is known as the Headless Horseman of Sleepy Hollow!

Into this sleepy little community came a new schoolmaster, Ichabod Crane. Appropriately named, he was tall and thin, with long skinny arms and legs. With one leg tucked up under his body, he could have easily been mistaken for a crane.

Ichabod made little money for his services, so local parents took turns letting the schoolmaster live with them. To earn extra money, he gave singing lessons to the young ladies of the community. He often had dinner with these pupils and their families.

After dessert, he and the women gathered around the fireplace to exchange marvelous and frightening ghost tales. In particular, they told tales of the Headless Horseman.

The excitement of the stories, however, turned into terrifying memories during Ichabod's walk home. Ichabod trembled at dark shadows and unrecognizable shapes. He would freeze, listening for galloping hooves. Then, realizing it was only the wind in the trees and not the Headless Horseman, he would continue on his way.

Ichabod had a secret wish. He longed to live in one of the valley's huge farmhouses, and he hoped to marry into a family who owned one. One of Sleepy Hollow's wealthy farmers had a daughter who was not yet married, and Ichabod gave her singing lessons. Ichabod was determined to make this student, Katrina Van Tassel, his wife.

Unfortunately for Ichabod, Katrina already had a suitor. He was tall, with a huge chest and muscular arms. His name was Brom Van Brunt; but, because of his great strength, his friends called him Brom Bones.

Everybody loved Brom, and he loved practical jokes and pranks. When the local folks awoke at midnight and heard horses galloping past their farmhouses, they smiled at the whooping and hollering and exclaimed, "There goes Brom Bones and his gang!"

A silent feud arose between Brom and the schoolmaster as they competed to win Katrina's hand. Ichabod tried to impress Katrina with his intellect and singing, while Brom tried to embarrass Ichabod.

One sunny autumn day, a messenger arrived at the schoolhouse and invited Ichabod to a party that evening at the Van Tassel farmhouse. Ichabod dismissed school early and ran all the way home. He shaved, washed, combed his hair, and put on his only suit and a wool hat, making certain he looked his very best.

Then he borrowed a horse and saddle from his host. Ichabod mounted Old Gunpowder, gave him a kick, and took off to the Van Tassel farm.

Shortly after Ichabod's arrival, Brom Bones rode up in front of the farmhouse and dismounted his horse, Daredevil.

The fiddler soon started the music, and Ichabod, believing himself to be a wonderful dancer, led Katrina to the dance floor. He bobbed and bounced. He twitched and turned and twirled. Meanwhile, watching the dancers, Brom Bones glared with jealousy.

When the dance ended, Ichabod joined a group of people on the porch who were telling tales of the Headless Horseman. Someone said that in the nightly search for his head, the ghost tied up his horse among the graves in the local churchyard.

The church stood on a small hill, where a nearby stream trickled over the road. Across the stream lay a wooden plank bridge, shaded by thick overhanging branches. Local folks agreed that this bridge was where the Headless Horseman was most often met.

Brom Bones joined the group and claimed that one evening he was overtaken by the Horseman, whom he challenged to a race. Brom and Daredevil were winning until the Horseman reached the wooden plank bridge, and the headless ghost vanished in a pillar of fire!

Ichabod listened intently to the stories until the party broke up. As the guests began to leave, the schoolmaster lingered behind. Tonight he intended to ask for Katrina's hand. Ichabod crept up to Katrina's side and whispered something to her. Startled, she squealed and quickly drew away from Ichabod!

Poor, embarrassed Ichabod turned red, scowled, and stomped out of the house. He quickly mounted Gunpowder, gave him a kick, and spurred the horse into action.

It was past midnight as Ichabod traveled toward his temporary home. As he thought of the evening's events, all the scary stories and ghostly tales began to return. He stopped, thinking he heard a whistle—but it was only the wind rushing through the trees. He heard a groan—but it was only two branches rubbing against each other.

And then, out of the shadows, there rose a huge, dark figure. It did not move.

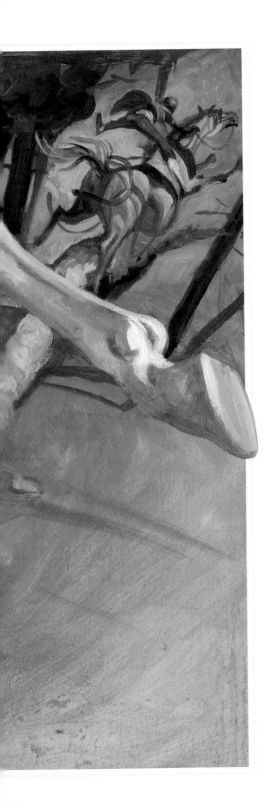

"Who, who are you?" Ichabod stammered.

Instead of answering, the shadowy figure slowly moved to the middle of the road. Ichabod could just make out the form of a large horse upon which towered a huge man covered with a dark flowing cloak.

Ichabod kicked Gunpowder and dashed forward, but the stranger stayed right behind him. Ichabod slowed his horse to a walk and the rider slowed also.

As the pair topped a hill, the silhouette of Ichabod's companion appeared clearly against the sky. Ichabod's eyes flew open in horror! His companion had no head! And the head which should have rested on the horseman's shoulders instead rested on his saddle!

Ichabod kicked and whipped and yelled at Gunpowder. Away they dashed, the ghost matching stride for stride. Stones flew! Sparks flashed!

The riders now approached the road to Sleepy Hollow, but Gunpowder bolted toward the opposite road. This road led across the wooden plank bridge and up the hill to the church with its graveyard.

Filled with panic, Ichabod suddenly felt his saddle slipping off. He grabbed Gunpowder around the neck as the saddle slipped to the ground and the ghostly horse trampled it.

Ahead, through the trees, Ichabod could see the church. Gunpowder pounded over the bridge. Ichabod turned around, expecting the ghost to disappear. Instead, the ghost stood up in his stirrups and hurled his head at Ichabod!

The schoolmaster tried to dodge the missile but was hit and fell to the ground. Then the ghostly rider and horses thundered past like a whirlwind.

Sunrise found Gunpowder, without saddle or bridle, outside his master's gate. Ichabod could not be found. After searching the area, local folks found the trampled saddle on the road leading to the church. Beyond the bridge, they found Ichabod's hat, and close by they found a shattered pumpkin.

Gossipers said the schoolmaster had left Sleepy Hollow because he was terrified of the ghost and he was embarrassed about losing his sweetheart. Katrina married Brom Bones, who always burst into laughter at the mention of the pumpkin, and some people believed he knew more than he was telling.

But the old country wives believe the schoolmaster was spirited away by supernatural means. And those who pass the bridge on a warm summer evening often fancy they hear the voice of the schoolmaster singing a melancholy tune amid the quiet breezes of Sleepy Hollow.

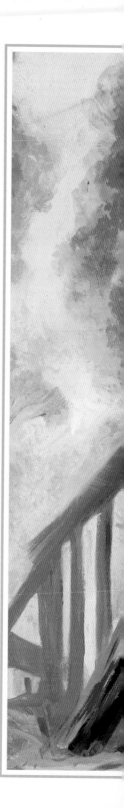

Washington Irving

(1783-1859)

Born in New York City, Washington Irving was the youngest of eleven children. As a boy, he explored much of the New York countryside, which later served as a backdrop for his folktales.

By the time Irving was twenty-six, he was a well-established writer in both the states and in Europe, but he did not use his own name on his work until he was in his fifties. His many pseudonyms were Jonathan Oldstyle, Launcelot Wagstaffe, and Friar Antonio Agapida. *The Legend of Sleepy Hollow* first appeared in his collection of stories entitled *The Sketch Book of Geoffrey Crayon*.

Irving was the first American author to receive widespread critical acclaim abroad as well as at home, fulfilling his lifelong dream of creating American folklore. The sales of his popular stories brought him a handsome fortune. He died in Tarry Town, New York, and was posthumously elected to the American Hall of Fame in 1900.